Who Will Carve the Turkey This Thanksgiving?

Jerry Pallotta

SCHOLASTIC INC.
New York   Toronto   London   Auckland
Sydney   Mexico City   New Delhi   Hong Kong

David Biedrzycki

Dear Mom,
Thank you for the stuffed mushrooms, the lentil soup, the artichokes,
the lobster ravioli, the homemade cranberry sauce, the turkey,
the baked vegetables, the cider, the pumpkin pie, the coffee Jell-O,
the pecan pie, and the pizzelles.
Love, Jerry

For Pat Meier, Walter Carmichael, Gary Brown, Nancy Sampson,
Carolyn Mesick, Kate Corkery, Lenore Piccoli, and Anne Marie Doyle.
Thanks for *giving* me the opportunity to speak at your schools.
— D.B.

ISBN-13: 978-0-545-14773-5
ISBN-10: 0-545-14473-6

Text copyright © 2009 by Jerry Pallotta
Illustrations copyright © 2009 by David Biedrzycki
All rights reserved. Published by Scholastic Inc.
SCHOLASTIC and associated logos are trademarks and/or registered trademarks of Scholastic Inc.

12 11 10 9 8 7 6 5 4 3 2 1   9 10 11 12 13 14/0

Printed in Singapore   46

First printing, October 2009

Today is Thanksgiving!

Mom always cooks a wonderful meal.

But who will carve the turkey this year?

A killer whale would be a good choice.

But why is it staring at me? Yikes!

Maybe Mom could use a saber-toothed tiger.

But they are extinct. We'll never find one.

And how about a Tyrannosaurus rex?

No! They probably never brush their teeth.

A polar bear could carve the turkey with one swipe

But WHAP! Its paw might knock it out the window.

A great white shark would be perfect.

But it would scare the whole house!

Leafcutter ants could carve the turkey.

But who wants to eat a zillion tiny slices?

Huge elephant tusks are too smooth!

And the elephant might eat all the stuffing!

I know! Piranhas are a possibility.

But they would want my fingers and toes for dessert.

Mom could ask a swordfish to carve the turkey.

Watch out! He'll cut the table in half!

What are you doing, sneaky coyote?

Bring that turkey back, RIGHT NOW!

We could ask a sea lion.

That's silly! Stop balancing the turkey on your nose.

A hippo has too big of a belly,

a skunk is too smelly, and

a moose would tip over the cranberry jelly.

Hey—look who's here! I guess that settles it.

Grandpa will carve the turkey—just like every year.

Happy Thanksgiving!